Soapstone
Porcupine

Soapstone Porcupine

Jeff Pinkney

illustrations by
Darlene Gait

ORCA BOOK PUBLISHERS

Library and Archives Canada Cataloguing in Publication

Pinkney, Jeffrey R. (Jeffrey Richard), 1962-, author
Soapstone porcupine / Jeff Pinkney ; illustrated by Darlene Gait.
(Orca echoes)

Issued in print and electronic formats.
ISBN 978-1-4598-1472-1 (softcover).—ISBN 978-1-4598-1473-8 (PDF).—
ISBN 978-1-4598-1474-5 (EPUB)

I. Gait, Darlene, 1968-, illustrator II. Title. III. Series: Orca echoes
PS8631.I535S59 2018   jC813'.6   C2017-904551-2
c2017-904552-0

First published in the United States, 2018
Library of Congress Control Number: 2017949719

Summary: In this early chapter book, a young Cree soapstone carver
and his dog learn about a porcupine after an unfortunate encounter.

Orca Book Publishers gratefully acknowledges the support for its publishing programs
provided by the following agencies: the Government of Canada through the Canada Book
Fund and the Canada Council for the Arts, and the Province of British Columbia
through the BC Arts Council and the Book Publishing Tax Credit.

Cover artwork and interior illustrations by Darlene Gait
Author photo by Julie Gagné

ORCA BOOK PUBLISHERS
www.orcabook.com

Printed and bound in Canada.

21 20 19 18 • 4 3 2 1

To the dogs who wander into our lives and keep us

A Miss and A Wish:
A New Way to Shoot

The dog showed up the way snow does on a winter's day. She just drifted in and stayed.

"Half husky and half Lab, by the look of her," Dad says.

She's not old but not a puppy either. Her fur is so thick she does not like to be inside.

My big brother and I still haven't come up with a name we can both agree upon.

Until we do, we've been calling her *Atim*. That is the Cree word for "dog."

When we leave for school, she dances us good morning. When we get home in the afternoon, she's waiting for us with tail wagging. When my brother shoots pucks, she chases them and sometimes brings them back. When I take a walk along the river she is right there alongside.

"That's the first I've known a stray to wander this far down the tracks from town," Mom says.

We asked around to see if anyone was missing a dog. Mom and Dad took her to the veterinarian, got her shots and bought her a collar.

"Does that mean we can keep her?" my brother and I ask.

"I think the question is," Mom says,
"will she keep us?"

Atim and I are out on the front porch thinking things over. It's my birthday and I'm excited that Stan is on his way for a visit. Stan is my mom's cousin. They grew up together like brother and sister. Stan and my dad are buddies too. They like to do all kinds of things, especially fish and hunt.

But for me, there is a nervous feeling mixed in with all this springtime excitement. Last fall I went hunting for the first time with a real shotgun. I wasn't sure if Stan and Dad noticed that I missed a snow goose on purpose. The snow goose was in my sights. I'm a really good shot, but something inside me made me move the barrel and miss. Hunting is such a big part of my family's life. I am feeling scared about going hunting again. It is

all sitting on me like a big fat goose on an egg.

Here on the porch, Atim doesn't seem to have any worries, but she seems to know that I do. She has pressed her muddy self beside me and won't leave me alone. I guess Atim is becoming a real best friend.

Stan arrives with a big package under his arm.

"Package? What package?" Stan says. "I'm just here for a piece of cake."

Dad cooked my favorite meal. It's his famous Irish stew. Everyone starts singing "Happy Birthday." To me, of course. On the last line, when folks sing the words *to you*, Stan breaks into a great wolf howl, and we all join in. When it goes quiet we hear Atim outside the door, howling along, and everyone laughs. Mom sets down a vanilla-and-caramel cake with ten candles ablaze.

I close my eyes and wish that Atim will decide to keep us. Then I huff and puff and blow out all the candles with one mighty breath.

"*Mahkitonew*," jokes my brother.

He has just called me a bigmouth in Cree.

"I guess that means there won't be any left for you," I say to him with a smirk.

"Ha-ha," he says, but he does look worried that I might just mean it.

I get cards and presents. Even from my brother. He gives me a heavy package wrapped in crumpled newspaper with a sedge-grass ribbon. It's a piece of raw soapstone, the biggest chunk I've ever had!

"I found it by the riverbank after hours and hours of looking. I tested it for softness with my knife just like you showed me."

"Thank you. It's totally awesome. It will be my next carving."

In that package from Stan there is a new gun for me. Except it doesn't shoot ammunition. It shoots pictures! Stan got a special camera for me and mounted it on a gunstock. A gunstock is the wooden handle of a shotgun or a rifle. The shutter button on this camera is wired to where your trigger finger goes. When you pull the trigger a picture is taken. I can unhook the camera from the gunstock if I want and wear it around my neck.

"Great hunters don't just shoot guns," Stan says. "You have such a good aim. I want you to keep coming out to shoot with us." Then he leans over and whispers, "You won't miss on purpose with this." He winks and smiles, and Dad smiles too.

After supper Stan and Dad show me how to use the camera gun. Mom says I can use her computer to store all my pictures.

"Now get out and practice," Stan says. "It's just a few weeks till the hunt, and your new job is to take lots of pictures for the history books."

As I hold my new camera, my worries hatch and fly away. Now I can't wait to go hunting again with Dad, Stan and my brother. But instead of being a gun shooter, I'm going to be a camera shooter.

Sidekicks and Signs:

A Quandary of Quills

A gray jay dive-bombs and lands on Atim's back. The bird picks a loose thread from Atim's collar and pulls. Aim, zoom, *click*—I photograph the camp robber in the act. Atim does not seem to mind. Off the gray jay flies with the thread in its beak. Maybe it will knit a scarf for its fledglings.

We are out on the trails around our tourist lodge. Folks come here by train.

They bring binoculars and telescopes and cameras. Mom and Dad take them out on the river and into the marshlands.

"Our guests are for the birds," my joking dad says.

At the river crossing I practice focusing my camera where the bridge trestles meet the water. I pretend that the trestles are the legs of a great bridge monster who sees Atim and wants to play. The bridge monster shakes like a wet dog. A million birds swoop from under his belly while I get pictures of it all. Soon the herons and the sand-hill cranes will come back to the river. I will take lots of pictures of them too.

Next we walk through the grassy meadow where an osprey aerie sits atop a high pole. Mother and Father Osprey are sprucing up their nest.

I pretend we are mice hiding in the dry grasses. I shoot some pictures from a mouse's-eye view.

The path takes us across the train tracks. I pause and look for Lindy the way I always do when spring is in the air. Lindy is a good friend of our family. When he visits, he makes carvings to sell to our guests. I have watched Lindy make carvings for my whole life. He is an elder, and he tells stories about all the birds and animals.

Last year Lindy gave me my very first piece of soapstone and showed me how to carve. I carved a bear cub. Before Lindy left our lodge for his yearly travels, he gave me three more pieces of soapstone. My carvings are of a beluga whale, a snow goose and an otter. When I tried carving soapstone

I more than just liked it. Carving soapstone felt like something I've always been meant to do. My brother says I'm obsessed, but it's not like that. Besides, I could say the same for him about hockey.

I use the zoom on my camera to see far up the tracks, but no Lindy. Winter is over, and that means he will visit soon. I can't wait to see him and show him my carvings.

The new piece of soapstone from my brother stays on my mind. I wonder what carving is inside. Lindy says that whatever the carving is going to be is already there inside the stone. He says that sometimes you might be given a sign and then you will know what to carve. A sign can be any way that the world gives you a message. Signs come to you when your thoughts mix with your senses. I keep myself open to the signs and whispers all around, just like Lindy taught me.

Way into the marshlands the beaver pond is quiet. I imagine that Atim and I are beavers inside the great lodge of sticks and mud. We relax in front of a big-screen television with a bowl of popcorn.

Into the forest we go, all senses alert. I pretend that I am the greatest hunter of all time. My sidekick, the wild winter wolf, walks with me. Sunlight streams through the new leaves of spring. A sign reaches the great hunter. It is a scent carried on the breeze. The hunter stops, crouches. The scent becomes a stench. The hunter's nostrils flare. Only one creature has a smell like that. The hunter spots a slight movement.

He sees the outline of his prey. It is on the trunk of an aspen tree, a few feet off the ground.

There, in all its magnificence, is the wild Canadian porcupine. A coat of quills stands on guard. A tail full of sharp needles hangs ready to strike should the hunter make the mistake of getting too close.

The hunter calls to his sidekick in Cree. "*Âštam*," he says quietly. "Now sit, stay, good girl." The loyal wolf obeys the soft commands.

The porcupine comes into the hunter's crosshairs and into focus. When in shooting range there is no time to waste. The great hunter takes aim. But wait. The animal turns its head. White quills make a strange wiggly stripe along one side of its face. The hunter

can see the glimmer of a porcupine eye opening wide. Eyes of hunter and prey meet and hold fast to each other, but who is the more curious?

The hunter breaks the staring contest and gets in three rapid shots. *Click, click, click.* Then the hunter moves in closer. The porcupine stiffens. The animal sounds a high-pitched growl and lashes its tail.

All of a sudden the winter wolf flies by the great hunter, lips pulled back in a snarl. There is another lash of the porcupine's tail, followed by a great yelp of pain.

Oh no! This isn't pretend anymore.

Atim rolls on her back with paws to her muzzle and yelps. The porcupine climbs higher in the tree. Atim thrashes her head from side to side. I see porcupine quills sticking out from her snout. Atim digs at her snout with her paws. She yelps even louder at the pain this causes.

Atim is hurt. She thought the porcupine was going to hurt me. She was just trying to protect me. It's my fault. I want to run, and I want to hide, and I want to stop Atim's pain. And I just want to turn the clocks of the world back to before this happened.

Then I remember what Stan and Dad have taught me about hunting. When there is an emergency, always try to control your own panic first. So that is what I try to do.

I set down my camera. I kneel down beside Atim. I try to keep her paws away from her muzzle and her muzzle away from me. I notice that she cannot close her mouth because some quills are stuck inside.

"It's okay," I tell her. "It's just some silly porcupine quills. Thank you for helping me. Thank you for being so brave." My heart is racing. I try to speak calmly and it seems to help both of us.

I look up high in the tree, and there is the porcupine, looking down at us. Its quills have relaxed and lie flat. The strong scent is also calming down. I can see the wiggly stripe on the animal's face. I know I will recognize this porcupine if I ever see it again.

I hold Atim's collar in one hand and pick up my camera with the other.

"Âštam," I say. "I will take you home now, Atim. Mom and Dad will know what to do."

As Atim runs along beside me, she whimpers and yelps in confusion

and pain. I feel the salty sting of tears in my eyes. I am crying too.

As we get close to home Atim's yelping brings Mom, Dad and my brother out to the porch. Dad runs to us. He takes Atim by the collar and leads her to the porch.

Mom looks at Atim's snout. "She must have forty quills in her face. This will be very painful for Atim. You must keep talking gently to the dog and hold her tightly."

Mom gets on the phone with the veterinarian. She comes back outside with some written notes and her first-aid kit. "Atim would have to wait too long to get to the veterinarian. We are going to help her."

Dad gets Atim to lie down on her side. He straddles the dog to hold her in place. Mom makes Atim swallow some medicine. My brother is sent to get Dad's needle-nose pliers and work gloves. I am sent to get an old pillow to place under Atim's neck.

Dad keeps holding Atim. My brother and I hold her paws so she does not swipe her face. Mom soaks the needle-nose pliers in hydrogen peroxide and pats them dry with a cotton ball. The medicine starts to make Atim groggy. Dad puts on his thick leather gloves to hold Atim's mouth open.

Even when groggy, Atim is very strong. She yelps and struggles each time Mom grabs a quill with the pliers. One by one the quills come out of Atim's mouth and snout. When each quill is pulled, drops of blood stain her furry muzzle.

When about a dozen quills are left sticking out of Atim's muzzle, Mom says it's time to switch. She takes my place holding Atim's paws, and I take the pliers. Dad gives me a nod.

"Grip the quill like you saw me do," Mom says. "Pull it straight back. Pull it like you mean it. Check to make sure you get the whole quill. Then get going on the next one."

Mom sure makes it look easy. You have to pull hard because each quill has barbs like a fish hook. Each time I reach with the pliers I feel Atim flinch. She knows it's going to hurt, and I can almost feel it with her. I'm crying too, but I don't let my feelings stop me from doing a good job for Atim.

My brother takes a turn as well. Dad and Mom and I hold Atim for him.

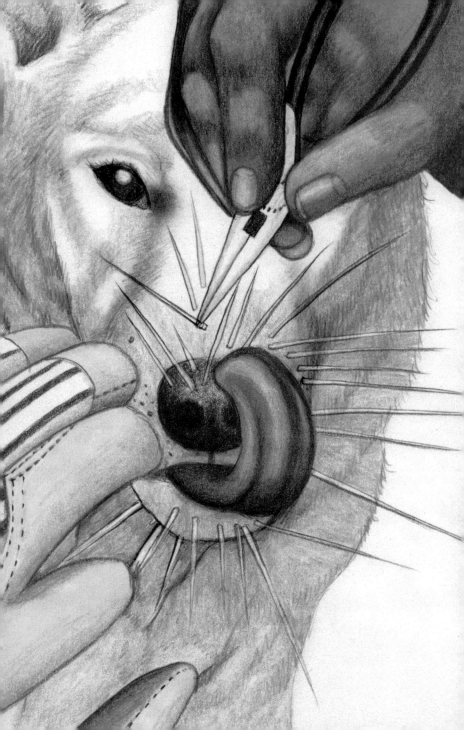

He is scared like I was. I can tell by his eyes that he can feel Atim's pain too, but there is also anger in his eyes.

Mom uses a cloth to pat Atim's snout and gently wash her muzzle. We do a final check to make sure all the quills are out. Atim is calmer now but still whimpers and tries to bury her nose between her paws.

When I had my worries Atim would not leave my side. So today I stay with her to make her feel calm and make sure she does not paw at her swollen face. I keep telling her how brave she is and I thank her for protecting me in the forest.

Supper is late. Everyone is upset for the poor dog. My brother is still upset after we are tucked into our room for the night.

"A lot of good your camera gun did for Atim," my brother says through the darkness. "I'll find the porcupine who hurt her. And my gun doesn't shoot pictures!"

I don't know what to say back to him, so I don't say anything. The silence in our room becomes very loud. I lay awake long after my brother's breathing turns to sleep.

Hunters, Hunger and Hopeful Hearts:
A Shot in the Dark?

Mom points with her face to the north. The tracks stretch out like a giant ladder that leans against the horizon. What Mom points at is only a little dot at first. The little dot grows slowly into the shape of a man walking. He is bent under the weight of a sack slung over his shoulder.

"He's here, he's here!" I yell and take off up the tracks.

Lindy sees me running. He puts down his sack and bows to greet me. I give him a big hug. My nose fills with outdoor adventures I can't wait to hear about.

"I have my carvings to show you," I say. I tell him what they are, and I ask him how his winter was. Then I ask him what sort of things he is carving. I ask him how long he will stay. I ask him how things are to the north and if he has ever carved a porcupine. And then I realize I am talking so fast that he hardly has time to listen, let alone give me answers.

He just laughs his happy laugh and says, "I think you could be an auctioneer if you ever have enough of stone carving."

Lindy is a bit more bent over than I remember, and he walks a bit slower. But his eyes are as bright as ever and his laugh rings with the same happiness. We walk back to where Dad and my brother and some of our guests have joined Mom. Everyone cheers and greets Lindy.

"*Wachay*," Mom says. "Will you join us for supper?"

"*Meegwetch*," says Lindy with a nod.

Dad and my brother take Lindy's bags to his room. He says he will sit by the river until suppertime.

Then Lindy turns to me and says, "Please show me your carvings."

I run to my bedroom, reach under the bed, grab my special wooden box and run down to the riverbank.

Lindy studies each one. The butterflies in my stomach are flying loop-de-
loops. Finally, he speaks.

"You are a stone carver. Tell me
about your signs and whispers and how
you knew these carvings were inside the
stone."

I tell him about the beluga whale on a canoe trip with Mom. About hunting with Dad, Stan and my brother. About missing on purpose when I shot at the snow goose and how much I worried about that. I tell him how I'm going to be a camera shooter now. About how I met the otters this past winter and how they went whooshing down the riverbank. I think I tell him all I've ever had to tell. It's dusk when Mom calls us in for supper.

Lindy hardly has time to eat a mouthful with all the excited questions and the laughter at the table.

Bedtime comes too soon.

Lindy joins us for breakfast. My brother has decided to spend his

Saturday out hunting. I know what he is after. It is no surprise that the talk at the table is about poor Atim and the porcupine.

"I once walked with a dog who tried to bite *kâko*," Lindy says. "Many quills got stuck in his face. Just like your Atim, he whined and whimpered very loudly while I pulled them out."

"Have you ever hunted a porcupine?" my brother asks Lindy.

"One winter long ago, my mother, my father, my sister and I became weak with hunger. My father sent me out to hunt kâko. At the end of that cold day, I turned my back to the setting sun and saw the quills reflected high in a pine tree. I promised kâko never to hunt him again if he would feed my family.

We ate for the first time in days. My father pulled many quills from my hand that day."

"How did it feel to have quills stuck in you?"

"I also whined and whimpered very loudly."

"Why did you promise to leave him alone?"

"Many hunters choose to hunt kâko only when they are very hungry and other food is scarce. Those hunters believe that if you take kâko when you are not in great hunger, kâko may not be there when you are."

My brother is quiet. After breakfast he leaves with his rifle, Atim and the lunch Dad packed for him.

Lindy invites me to the riverbank to carve with him.

I feel sad about what my brother is doing. I also wonder what Atim will do if she faces the porcupine again.

But you can't be with Lindy and not be in a happy mood. Sometimes when he laughs, it's like his whole face disappears into its wrinkles. We spend many hours together when he visits. He knows things about the animals that you can only know from being outside with them and watching them closely for many hours and days and years. I have lots of questions for him, especially about porcupines.

"Have you ever carved a soapstone porcupine?"

"A long time has passed since my signs have brought me kâko in the stone."

I tell him about the smell when I snuck up to take the pictures.

"If you could smell the porcupine, it means you are not as sneaky as you think. That smell means kâko knew you were there."

"The scent was like a mix of spring swamp, summer ga*rbage and my brother's hockey bag when he forgets to air it out.*"

"*To the porcupine's sweetheart, that smell is like a bouquet of roses.*" *Lindy laughs*, and so do I.

"Why didn't the porcupine run away?" I ask.

"Kâko seldom runs. When kâko walks, he slowly sways from side to side, like he hasn't a care in the world."

"Is that because of the quills?"

Lindy nods. "Kâko is very brave in his own coat. He knows he is well protected. He can be curious about

what other creatures are doing, but he will not be pushed to change his actions or his mind."

Lindy looks at the soapstone my brother gave me. "Your brother is a real prospector. He has found a good piece of carving stone."

As I sit with Lindy, I begin work on my soapstone porcupine. I also watch Lindy carve. He works as if he has eyes in his fingers. Where there was just an edge of raw stone, a paw or a beak or a wing will be formed. Sometimes a lot of time goes by before any words are said between us. But I always feel welcome. He shows me that he knows I am there by making sure I can see his hands and what he carves.

The day slips by as all the best days do. When we go in for supper, my brother is not yet back from his day of hunting. As darkness falls, the loudest thing at our table is the empty plate at his spot.

Dad looks worried.

Mom does not.

"He is a good woodsman, and he knows his way," she says to Dad.

But Dad wants to go look for him. He is starting to get ready when we hear a faint bark from outside. Mom is the first one to the door.

We all go out to the porch.

There is my brother, returning on the river path with Atim at his side. My brother has not brought home any kill. No one asks about that.

Mom gives my brother a big hug. "Come, eat," she says. "I have held a warm supper. You will not go hungry in this house."

The night ends as it usually does, with my brother and me tucked into our room.

"Does your kâko have a stripe down one side of his face?"

"Yes," I say. "That is the one."

"He was in my sights just at dusk, high in a poplar tree. I was ready to take him. I told him I did not like what he did to Atim."

"And then what?"

"I told him that I will not shoot my gun today. I told him that I will wait until I am very hungry and that now I know how to find him."

I fall asleep with pride in my heart for my brother. But I decide he doesn't have to know it.

Carving Tools and Tourists:
You Can't Push a Porcupine!

Most folks board the train way to the south, where the roads end and the train tracks begin. Lindy and I are boarding for the last leg of the journey north. The train stops here just for us. Conductor Gillian is at the open door. She is a friend of Mom's. Lindy is taking the train into town to carve for the tourists for a few days. He has invited me to join him for the first day.

Mom and Dad said it was okay! I will ride home all by myself. I have never done that before. The butterflies in my stomach swarm with excitement.

The train is warm and it rumbles and creaks. It is full of the sounds families and friends make when they are excited about a big adventure.

The engineer blasts his horn long and loud as the train rolls into town. The station is bustling with travelers. Long ago, ships sailed here from France and England to trade for beaver pelts. Now tourists come to see the historic sites and to learn what it's like to be Cree. Tourists also come here on canoe trips or to fish and hunt. Of course, lots of folks come to see the birds. The river is much wider here than where it passes by our lodge. We are so close now to where the river spills into the ocean that the river rises and falls with the tides.

Lindy leads us near the town docks to where three other people sit along the shoreline. I see that they are carving soapstone. They are very happy to see Lindy. Lindy introduces me.

Silas and Rose have come from the far northwest. Rose was born and raised here. She travels back with Silas every year. Silas shapes a beaver out of a piece of very dark stone. Rose carves a loon. They have carvings on display for tourists to buy.

"I come up from down east way," Pierre says.

Pierre works with a large piece of brownish stone. He holds out his carving to me. It is an owl. He is working on

the curved back and on forming the tail feathers. It is a beautiful carving. Beside Pierre are carvings of a walrus and an osprey. Pierre speaks French to the tourists who come by.

Lindy unties the ribbon from his tool roll and spreads it out. The canvas has pouches that hold a set of rasp files, a well-worn jackknife and a beeswax candle for polish. He lays out his finished pieces beside him. He has two bear cubs, a beaver, a raccoon and a narwhal. Lindy begins to shape a new piece of stone.

I unwrap my carving stone from the soft rags Mom gave me. I place my rasp file and my jackknife in front of me on a piece of cloth. I can hardly believe I am here with a group of carvers, and that today I am one of them.

We get a lot of attention. Most folks approach shyly or watch from a distance. Some folks are not shy at all. Almost everyone takes pictures. I am wearing my camera around my neck and I take some pictures too.

Rose looks at my carving. "I like how you have chosen to make your porcupine with the quills down. It gives me a much calmer feeling than if the quills were up for a fight."

My porcupine holds on to a tree trunk just like in my pictures. Pierre shows me how to use the tip of my knife blade to make the tree bark look real. Lindy shows me how to carve the porcupine's claws so they look like they cling to the tree.

Two giggly teenage girls sit down, one on either side of me. The girls ask if they can take a selfie with the three of us in it.

"Okay," I say and hold up my carving as they squeeze in for the picture.

Pierre gives me a big wink and laughs. I laugh too—and blush.

A tourist wants to buy one of Lindy's bear cubs but thinks the price is too high. He offers less money than what Lindy is asking.

Lindy laughs his friendly laugh and says, "Okay, but at that price I will take off the back leg and the tail." The tourist laughs also and then gives Lindy his full price.

Sometimes folks say things like, "Hey, kid, whatcha workin' on?"

I smile and say, "Work in progress," but I move my hands like Lindy does so they can see what I am carving. My porcupine is almost finished. I have shaped the head, body and tail. Lindy has shown me how to polish the carving first and then etch the stone to show the porcupine quills.

Silas and Rose have a sack filled with chunks of dark-gray stone. Their polished carvings are jet black with beautiful lines and light shining through. Lindy shows some of the white stone he collects from his secret locations. Silas picks up a piece. Lindy nods and accepts a piece of dark-gray soapstone in return. Pierre has some of his reddish-brown stone for trading. Now I know how Lindy gets so many types of carving stone in his sack.

Dad packed a big lunch before the train left this morning. We have enough to share with Silas, Rose and Pierre. I don't know how Dad knew to pack so many extra sandwiches. He can be pretty smart sometimes.

The afternoon flies by. Freighter canoes zip back and forth like big green water bugs. Barges swim like giant beavers with loads of lumber. Waves dance sideways and wash like drum rolls against the rocky shoreline. The breeze off the river is misty and cool and feels good under the warm sun. The sky is big and blue and busy. Ospreys swoop and soar, and loon calls can be heard in the distance. Seagulls circle, sound and dive-bomb. High overhead, a great blue heron crosses the bright sky.

Here on land, pickup trucks and all-terrain vehicles kick up dust. Stray dogs weave through the traffic and the traffic weaves through the dogs. I watch for dogs who might be brothers and sisters of Atim. Excited groups of tourists rubberneck in all directions. Those who forgot to put on bug spray, slap and smack and do "the dance of the tasty newcomer." Windbreakers are bright and sun hats are wide brimmed. You can hear excited and happy words in lots of languages. There are so many wonderful things to see and do that folks come here from all over the world. The river rises with the tidewater, swelling with pride.

My finishing touch is to carve a wiggly stripe on one side of my porcupine's face. I am very proud that some tourists have asked if they could buy it, but I don't feel like I want to sell.

Lindy sees that I wonder about that.

"It is okay to say no," he says. "Your signs will tell you if it is the right thing to do."

Crowds of people arrive at the docks to make their way back up to the waiting train. I wrap up my carving, pack up my tools and load my pack for the journey home.

Pierre takes a last look at my soapstone porcupine. "I love the way this porcupine is looking sideways with such curiosity. I have seen him many times in the forest," he says.

"Looks like we have a real up-and-comer here," Silas says to Lindy.

"As soon as this young carver starts to sell his work, that's it for me—no more business!" says Pierre with a fake frown, and everyone laughs.

Rose hands me a small piece of her dark-gray soapstone to keep. Silas gives me a thumbs-up.

"Thank you," I say. "It was really cool to meet you both."

Pierre reaches to shake my hand. "This is to say thanks for the great lunch," he says. In my hand he places a piece of his carving stone. It will polish to a shiny brown with reddish swirls. I am excited to have it.

"*Merci beaucoup*," I reply.

Lindy walks me back up to the train station. He will be staying in town for a couple of days to carve with Silas, Rose and Pierre before he visits again at our lodge. Already I can't wait. I reach to shake Lindy's hand but then change my mind and give him a hug instead.

"Meegwetch," I say to Lindy. "Today was so awesome."

"Thank you also," he says. "You are learning to trust your signs and your hands too. I am very proud of you."

Conductor Gillian greets us. "It's your lucky day," she says. "You get to sit with me."

Gillian has her papers spread out at the back of the passenger car. She makes room for me. The train pulls out of the station with a goodbye blast of its horn. I wave through the window. Lindy smiles and waves back. The bustling town becomes the backs of houses, then cabins, then the quiet sway of sedge grass.

Conductor Gillian asks me how my day went. She listens to my stories about carving for the tourists. I show her my photos. Gillian laughs at the one I took of those teenage girls taking pictures of themselves. And then I show her my soapstone porcupine.

"I like the way you made the tail swing sideways rather than hang straight down. It's the touch of a master carver to show movement in solid stone. You are certainly good enough to sell your work to the tourists."

"But I didn't want to sell my carving like the others were doing."

"Why not?" asks Gillian.

"I think if I had any money, I would just want to buy this carving back."

Gillian smiles and turns my carving in her hands. "Did anyone take your picture with the carving?"

"Lots of tourists did."

"Those photographs are a good way to share your work and keep it too."

"I never thought of it that way. Most folks wanted me to hold up my carving for their pictures."

"Just one day on the job, and you are already the world-famous boy with the soapstone porcupine!" We laugh, but I am proud too.

She sets my soapstone porcupine on the small table in front of our seats. "I'll be right back," she says as she stands up. "I have to punch the tickets."

Gillian heads down the aisle. Just then a hand reaches over and snatches up my carving.

"How much do you want for this?" asks a fast-talking lady in a neon-red windbreaker. She is thin and wiry with a pointy face like a marten or a fisher.

I am too startled to speak, but she keeps talking anyway.

"I said, how much money? I must have it."

"That carving is not for—" and then I swallow the rest of what I am saying from nervousness.

"Nonsense," she cuts in. "I didn't see any of these in the souvenir shop. You must have got the last one."

"That is not from a store." My voice is very weak.

"Speak up, boy. What do you mean, *not from a store?*"

"I carved it myself," I manage to say, wishing Lindy or Stan or Mom or Dad or even my brother was with me.

"Ha-ha, very funny. A kid like you couldn't carve like this! How much? Name your price."

She roughly turns the carving over and over in her hands. It feels like my

heart is beating inside that soapstone porcupine. I think that if I were a porcupine, I would have my quills up right now. And then I think of how the porcupine knows it is well protected so it can be brave. I think of how the porcupine does not let itself be pushed around.

I say, "I'm sorry, but that soapstone carving is already spoken for." I put my hands out and look right into her eyes. I try to smile, but my lips are shaky.

The lady arches her eyebrows like she's going to say something else. She pauses, narrows her eyes and then sets the carving back into my outstretched hands. She squeezes up her face and stomps away. I hold my carving tightly. It takes a few minutes for my quills to relax. I wrap up the porcupine and carefully tuck it back into my pack.

When I told that lady the carving was spoken for, I did not tell a fib. At that moment I made a decision about it. The soapstone porcupine is going to be a gift from me to my brother. I am so proud of him for respecting the real live porcupine that I am going to give him this one.

Conductor Gillian comes back from the far end of the passenger car. "Would you like to go up front to see the engineer and help drive the train?"

"You bet I would!"

"Okay!" she says. "I'll take you because I like to drive the train too."

"Hey, if it isn't one of the boys from the river crossing," the engineer says.

"Glad to have you on board."

When the train nears our stop and our platform comes into view, guess who is at the controls with the engineer and the conductor?

I can see the outline of my family on the platform to greet me. I wail the horn as I lean out the open window and wave.

Mom looks up and points.

Dad is laughing.

My big brother's mouth forms the words *No way!*

Atim is there too. Her tail wags with excitement. I am happy she has chosen to keep us. My birthday wish is coming true.

The steel wheels screech and squeal. The whole train makes a special stop

just for me. I am encircled by a family hug.

As the train rolls down the track, the caboose gently sways like a porcupine sways when it has no worries and is happy to be home.

Pronunciation Guide

When a Cree word appears, Moose Cree dialect is used.

âštam (ash-tum): come here
atim (a-tim): dog
kâko (ka-koh): porcupine
meegwetch (mee-gwetch): thank you
mahkitonew (mah-kee-tah-nayo): one with a big mouth
wachay (wah-chay): "what cheer" or "greetings" or "goodbye" (this word has many spellings, including *wah-chay, watchay, wachey, wâciye*)

Acknowledgments

The author offers sincere thanks to: editor Liz Kemp, for refinement and shine; Darlene Gait, for illustrative magic; the team at Orca, for presenting the story so well; Greg Spence, for advice about the Moose Cree language; and Rick MacLeod Farley and Russell Turner for insights. Heartfelt thanks also to family members: Leslie, for support beyond compare; Isabella, for youthful perspective; Maarika, for assuredness; June, for inclusiveness; Charlie, for orientation; Morley, for adherence; Gillian, for whom the conductor is named; and Alexandra, for literary reclamation and loosening the quill when it was stuck.

Jeff Pinkney likes to be out in a canoe or on his mountain bike on forest trails. He has met a few porcupines along the way. He is an amateur stone carver, having learned the art from a Cree elder who provided him with his first piece of soapstone. Jeff carved a bear cub. He also writes poetry and is a proud member of the Live Poets of Haliburton County. *Soapstone Porcupine* is the second novel in the Soapstone Signs series. The stories draw on Jeff's experiences while living and traveling as a development consultant in Canada's James Bay Frontier, where he acquired a deep appreciation for the people and the landscape. He knows firsthand what it's like to be a little brother and a big brother too. Jeff is husband to Leslie and father to Maarika, Alexandra and Isabella. Learn more at www.jeffpinkney.com.

Also by Jeff Pinkney

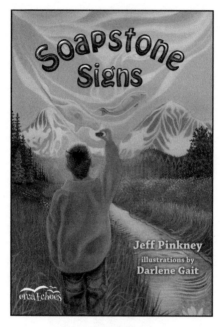

9781459804005 PB
9781459804012 PDF
9781459804029 EPUB

Only the carver knows the soapstone's true shape.

Soapstone Signs and Whispers:
A Spring Arrival

Lindy travels opposite to the geese. Every spring after the ice breaks up on the river, he walks in from the north along the tracks. Even though his name is Lindbergh, everyone calls him Lindy. Even me. He has a way of being polite without saying anything. He smells like campfires and the outdoors.

Lindy carries a big burlap sack of soapstone pieces. Folks ask where he's found all that soapstone. He just laughs and tells them, "Somewhere between here and there."

Our place is one of the stops on his yearly journey to the south. We operate the lodge between the river and the train tracks. Lindy trades his carving in return for a place to sleep and food to eat. Each year, Mom puts the one he carves for us in the glass display case. Our guests sometimes ask to buy them, but Mom always says, "Not these ones—they are special to us."

When someone asks, "Whatcha working on?" Lindy smiles and says, "Work in progress." He leaves his finished carvings on the ground beside him, and the tourists can look and touch and buy those ones if they want. He carves bears, loons, owls, ospreys, beavers, walrus, seals and even fish.

Lindy has a place he likes to sit by the riverbank. I like to sit with him and watch him carve. Sometimes he hands me what he is working on. I look and then hand it back without saying a word. Really, that is saying a lot.

Today, when Lindy finishes a carving, I become curious. "How do you know what you will carve next?"

He pauses, looking thoughtful. "You ask the stone," he says. "Whatever it is going to be, it is already there."

"How does the stone answer you?"

"Sometimes, you might be given a sign, and then you will know what to carve."

"Do you mean signs like the ones where the train stops?"

"Those are important signs too, but a sign can be any way that the world gives you a message. Signs come to you when your thoughts mix with your senses."

I know what all the senses are. I ask Lindy, "If you mix your thoughts with your sight, can you see what is inside the stone?"

He lifts the piece he is working on, turns his hand and studies it against the clouds. "Sometimes it feels like I can see into the stone."

"Does the stone talk to you?"

"Sometimes I feel like the stone is whispering to me."

"Can you ever tell by the smell and the taste?"

Lindy laughs. "Sometimes the smells and tastes of the world around me give me signs about what is inside the stone."

"Can you tell what is waiting inside by touching the stone?"

"Sometimes if I hold it just so, it's like I can feel what is inside."

"What if the stone won't tell you?"

Lindy reaches into his burlap sack and holds a small piece out to me. "This is for you—ask for yourself."

My very first piece of soapstone. It is dull gray and feels powdery before it is carved. I know from watching Lindy that the soapstone will look different after it is made into a carving. It will polish to a beautiful dark green with black swirls and white shimmers like the northern lights.

I am not sure my ears are sharp enough to hear the soapstone whisper. "Will you tell me what is inside, so I can try to carve it out?"

"That piece of stone has chosen you. Only the one who is to be the carver will know."

"What if it never tells me?"

He laughs again. "Take it with you and be ready for a sign."